TARA NORMAL

BOOK ONE: PALE HORSE

WRITTEN & ILLUSTRATED BY
HOWIE NOEL

Dedicated to Team Tara.

Edited by Jennifer Noel-Smith & Shelley Noeldechen

FOREWARD BY CHIP COFFEY

Howie Noel is anything but normal. And in my estimation, that is a good thing!

I first met Howie when we were both appearing at a paranormal conference. I was immediately impressed by his immense talent as an artist and as the weekend progressed, I was charmed by his offbeat sense of humor and his colorful, vivid imagination.

Tara Normal is a true labor of love for Howie. He has created a character – and her world – that is a testament to his brilliance and creativity. I predict that Howie will enjoy great success and that Tara will join the ranks of other beloved comic book heroes.

I am truly honored to call Howie my friend.

Howie Noel with Chip Coffey

Chip Coffey is an internationally acclaimed psychic, medium, spiritual counselor, paranormal investigator, and lecturer. In addition to starring in **Psychic Kids: Children of the Paranormal**, *he has made appearances on* **Paranormal State, Haunted Collector** *and* **Celebrity Ghost Hunt**

MEANWHILE, IN THE REAL WORLD...

Praise for a great comic by Dirk Manning

There's two lines of dialogue spoken by Tara Normal that really sum up the crux of what this series is about, as well as what raises it head-and-shoulders above so many of the other works out there – comic and otherwise – that also deal with paranormal problem-solvers.

The first line is this:
"Some people can play piano. Some people can paint.
I can see ghosts."

The line is brilliant in its simplicity. In Tara Normal, we meet a tough-as-nails heroine who approaches unworldly situations with that sort of pragmatic charm.

Not only can Tara see ghosts (and punch them out of existence when need be) but, as we learn pretty early in this tale, she's also proven to the whole world that they exist … and she expects you all to deal with it.

Or not.
Whatevs.

The second quote – and this is the one that really gets me – is this:
"My life's not all doom and gloom, though."

Mind you, this is coming from a woman who can see and talk to ghosts – and sometimes even has to fight them – but still can't connect with her departed mother.

Rather than let this horror-and-murder-filled world create a sense of angst and dread, Tara Normal (the character) and Tara Normal, (the book) instead offer us a scary, yet non-soul-crushing horror experience.

Make no mistake, folks, what you're about to indulge in (if you haven't already skipped ahead to the story itself, that is) is indeed an experience

Despite the dark central plot (ghosts are real and some of them are very capable of hurting us), the characters, the dialogue, and (especially) the art created by Howie Noel offers a non-gritty view of a world where, under a surface filled with happiness, joy, and humor lie a mysterious and at times deadly undercurrent of unexplainable mystery…

You know, just like in the real world.

Your friend in comics,
Dirk Manning

February 1, 2014

Dirk Manning is the writer of such comics (or books about comics) as **NIGHTMARE WORLD** *and* **LOVE STORIES TO DIE FOR** *(Image Comics),* **WRITE OR WRONG: A WRITER'S GUIDE TO CREATING COMICS** *(Caliber) and* **TALES OF MR. RHEE** *(Devil's Due), the latter of which even features a cameo towards the end that should be of interest to any of you who picked up this book. Dirk has also had the joy of collaborating with Howie on the past on projects such as* **TARA NORMAL** *and the one-shot comic* **AN INABILITY TO COPE…***, and considers himself very lucky to be a friend of such a talented creator. For more information about Dirk, visit www.DirkManning.com. Cthulhu is his homeboy.*

WHAT AN EXCELLENT DAY FOR AN EXORCISM.

WELCOME TO
SAINT CATHERINE
OF SIENA
HOSPITAL
FOR THE INSANE

WELCOME, FATHER. I CALLED YOU AS SOON AS I WAS NOTIFIED *13* WAS LOOSE.

HUH. MAYBE YOU SHOULD'VE CALLED ME SLIGHTLY EARLIER, DOCTOR.

NO. THIS IS IMPOSSIBLE. THIS-- THIS JUST *HAPPENED.*

OH MY GOD!

Present Day

THE  HON

70º F

POE COUNTY
LIFE FOR SOME

| HOME | NEWS | JUST THE MURDERS | LOCAL | SPORTS | LENORES | BUSINESS | PARANORMAL | CELEBRITY | HEALTH | MARKET | SERVICES |

TARA NORMAL ACTIVITY
LOCAL GHOST HUNTER PROVES GHOSTS EXIST

I WAS BORN WITH AN ADVANCED FORM OF CLAIRVOYANCE. I CAN SEE SPIRITS AND COMMUNICATE WITH THEM.

WHILE AT THE VATICAN, I DEVELOPED TECHNOLOGY TO SHOW OTHERS HOW I SEE THINGS. I INVITED PROMINENT SCIENTISTS AND SKEPTICS TO VIEW *MY DISCOVERY.*

A FUNNY THING HAPPENED WHEN THE WORLD LEARNED THE *TRUTH* ABOUT GHOSTS. THERE WAS NO MASS PANIC. NO MASS INSANITY.

THAT WAS *INSANE!*

THE DOWNSIDE IS THERE'S A LOT OF PEOPLE IN CONTROL WHO AREN'T HAPPY THAT THE TRUTH IS GETTING OUT. A SHADOW BRANCH OF THE GOVERNMENT IS AFRAID OF WHAT I'LL REVEAL NEXT.

THE BIGGEST THREAT TO THEIR CONTROL IS THE PEOPLE LEARNING THERE IS LESS TO FEAR IN THIS LIFE.

THE DRUNKEN POET

PEOPLE NOW KNOW THERE IS MORE TO THIS WORLD.

EVERYDAY I'M TAILED BY UNMARKED BLACK *SUVS* DRIVEN BY MEN IN BLACK WHO ARE TRYING TO LISTEN TO MY PHONE CALLS AND READ MY EMAILS.

YES.

SO NOW I'M FOLLOWED BY DEAD PEOPLE AND THESE CREEPERS.

I GUESS THAT MEANS WE'VE BEEN MADE?

I HAVE A FAMILY. MY DAD, *ABE NORMAL*, AND *HOGAN*, MY PUG. WE LIVE ABOVE MY DAD'S MAGIC SHOP.

DAD NEVER TRULY RECOVERED FROM MY MOM'S DEATH.

HI HOGAN!

MY MOM MAY HAVE DIED, BUT MY DAD'S THE ONE WHO BECAME A GHOST. HE'S ONLY A SAD MEMORY OF THE MAN HE WAS.

I ONLY PARTLY PUT THE BLAME ON HIS DRINKING. THE REAL CAUSE IS HIS BROKEN HEART.

MY MOM DIED UNDER *VERY* MYSTERIOUS CIRCUMSTANCES WHILE RESEARCHING HER FINAL NOVEL, *DEMONOLOGY*. I'VE SEARCHED FOR THE TRUTH EVER SINCE.

I DON'T KNOW, DAD. I'M SORRY. I HAVE TO GO.

TARA... WHY CAN'T... YOU SPEAK TO HER? MY SARAH...

DAD WILL ASK ME THAT EXACT SAME QUESTION EVERY DAY. I CAN'T BLAME HIM. HE HAS A DAUGHTER WHO CAN TALK TO THE DEAD. WHY CAN'T I TALK TO MY DEAD MOM?

JAKE BOOKED US A GHOST HUNT AT A RUNDOWN HOUSE ACROSS TOWN. THE REALTOR CALLED US FOR HELP CLAIMING THEIR CLIENT WOULDN'T MOVE IN UNTIL WE GOT RID OF WHATEVER WAS HAUNTING THE LOCATION. WE WEREN'T ABLE TO SPEAK TO THE NEW OWNER DIRECTLY.

OH YEAH. BY THE WAY, ALL OF *LITTLE SALEM* IS HAUNTED. LIKE SUPER HAUNTED. LIKE POLTERGEIST PARTS 1, 2 & 3 LEVEL OF HAUNTED. STARE AT YOUR TV AND SAY *"THEY'RE HERE"* LEVEL OF HAUNTED.

WHAM!

SOLD

HAWES REALTY GROUP
1/800 555 2341
let us take ya home.

CHECK THIS OUT, BOBBY! I'M GONNA GO INVESTIGATE THE REST OF THIS HALLWAY.

GOT IT! MAN, I HOPE THAT AWESOME CATCH GOT CAUGHT ON CAMERA, BRO.

SMACK!

THIS IS WEIRD. THIS BALL HAS *YOUR NAME* ON IT, JEREMY.

To Jeremy My son

#32

WHAT?! LET ME SEE IT.

HERE YOU GO, MAN. IT'S RIGHT ON THE FRONT THERE.

COLD...

DUDE, IT'S AUTOGRAPHED BY MY *DAD!* HE WAS A PITCHER IN THE MAJORS. HOW DID THIS GET HERE?! HE *DIED* 15 YEARS AGO.

WOW. I'VE NEVER SEEN SO MANY *ORBS!* HELLO? I'M NOT HERE TO HURT YOU.

WOAH! YOU'RE A BIG BOY, HUH? LEMME JUST GET SOME VIDEO OF YOU. **SMILE** FOR THE CAMERA, BROTHER.
OH MY **GOD**.
SKRASSSSH!

HELLO, MY LITTLE FRIEND.

YES. YOU DID AN EXCELLENT JOB. OUR *MASTER* WILL BE MOST PLEASED.

ONCE WE HAVE COLLECTED ENOUGH *SOULS*, WE WILL BE FREE TO ROAM *OUTSIDE* THIS CURSED ASYLUM. THE WORLD WILL BE OURS TO *HAUNT*.

IT SOUNDS LIKE THEY'RE GETTING SOME WICKED INTERFERENCE ON THE MICS IN THERE.

WHAT ARE YOU BITCHING ABOUT NOW, BOBBY? A *BASEBALL*? I DIDN'T PUT A BASEBALL IN THE HALLWAY. I'M *OUTSIDE* AT CRAFT SERVICES, MORON.

KKSSHH!

*ELECTRONIC VOICE PHENOMENA

GHOST
SOLDIERS

THE SEER

The Captain's Bar

YOU RIDE A BIKE BECAUSE OF SITUATIONS LIKE THIS, DON'T YOU? TO GET THE GIRL TO HOLD ON TO YOU?

YUP.

HOW COME WE'VE NEVER HUNG OUT AT YOUR APARTMENT BEFORE?

BODE

FOODS

SALE

"HONEST Ben Franklin's MAGIC FUN SHOP

MAGIC SHOWS

GAMES

CLOSED

BECAUSE EVER SINCE MY MOM DIED, MY DAD HAS HAD SOME REALLY BAD DAYS.

YOU DON'T HAVE TO WORRY ABOUT THAT WITH ME, TARA.

I'M NOT GOING TO JUDGE.

ON SECOND THOUGHT, I MAY DO A LITTLE JUDGING.

WHAT THE HELL?

YOU GUYS MISSED SOME CRAZY, COOL SHIT. IT WAS RAD.

TARA. I'VE QUIT DRINKING. AND IT'S ALL THANKS TO THE CHAT I HAD WITH YOUR SPECTRAL FRIEND HERE.

SHADOWMAN!

LIKE ALIEN AA? DOES THAT MAKE IT AAA? OR IS THAT THING A GHOST?

OH, I'M NO GHOST, MR. WESTON. I'M AN INTER-DIMENSIONAL TRAVELER. AND I'M ALSO TARA'S VERY FIRST BFF IN THIS WHOLE WIDE WORLD.

JUST LIKE ABE'S HAD A MOMENT OF CLARITY, I HAD ONE WHEN I FIRST MET TARA.

HELLO.

SO, YOU CAN *SEE* ME?!

OF COURSE I CAN SEE YOU.

WHO ARE YOU TALKING TO, TARA?

MY FRIEND *SHADOWMAN*, MOMMY. BUT YOU SCARED HIM AWAY.

ME? HOW COULD I SCARE A SHADOW PERSON?

SPECIAL LIKE 'HE AND I' TARA.

BUT HE'S RIGHT. YOU ARE SPECIAL.

SHADOWMAN SAID YOU'RE NOT LIKE ME AND HIM. WE'RE SPECIAL BECAUSE WE BOTH SEE THINGS.

SO. RAD.

WHAT? NO. HOLD UP. TIME OUT. WHAT THE HELL IS A *GHOST PLANET*?

IT'S LIKE A GHOST TOWN, BUT SUPER-SIZED.

I PICKED A HELL OF A DAY TO QUIT DRINKING.

THE DEMONIC ENTITY WANTS THE ENTIRE PLANET TO BE OVERRUN BY DESTRUCTIVE SPIRITS AND DEMONS. WE DIE SO THEY CAN LIVE AGAIN.

THIS IS WHAT YOU WERE PUT ON THIS PLANET FOR, TARA. TO SAVE IT.

THE ANONYMOUS TIP TO THE PILLOWS HOUSE WASN'T RANDOM AT ALL. IT'S PART OF A TRAIL OF BREADCRUMBS LEADING TO THE TRUTH.

WHO HAS BEEN LAYING DOWN THE PIECES TO THE PUZZLE THOUGH?

WE ARE ALL EQUAL WHEN WE ARE DEAD.
SOON, WE SHALL BE FREE AND YOU WILL BE THE GHOSTS IN OUR HOMES.
THE LIVING WILL ENVY THE DEAD.
YOU MAY KEEP JEREMY'S BODY. I ALREADY HAVE HIS SOUL.
HAHAHAHA HAHAHAHA
WHAT THE HELL IS THAT THING, TARA?
SO YOU SEE HIM TOO? I DON'T KNOW WHAT HE IS. WHAT I DO KNOW IS I'M GOING INTO THAT HOSPITAL TO KICK HIS CREEPY ASS.

I CAN'T DISSUADE YOU FROM GOING IN THERE, CAN I?

NOPE.

A BARRIER OF NEGATIVE ENERGY PERMEATES THE ENTRANCE OF THE HOSPITAL.

A HISTORY OF MADNESS AND SUFFERING SUFFOCATES THE ASYLUM'S HALLS. THIS PLACE SHOULD BE TORN DOWN. IT'S EVIL. PURE EVIL.

IT'S NOT A SURPRISE CONSIDERING HOW MANY PEOPLE DIED HERE...HOW MANY SOULS ARE TRAPPED INSIDE.

CREAK!

...

TO BE CONTINUED IN BOOK TWO:
FIGHT THE FALLEN

SAINT CATHERINE OF SIENA HOSPITAL FOR THE INSANE

KILLER CARICATURES & ORIGINAL ART
STARTING AT $19⁹⁹

The Walking Dead's
Norman Reedus

UNIQUE ORIGINAL ART • EASY ONLINE ORDERING • PERFECT GIFTS

SAINT CATHERINE OF SIENA
HOSPITAL FOR THE INSANE

LITTLE SALEM, MD

ADMISSION FORM

LAST NAME	FIRST NAME

REASON FOR ADMISSION

- ☐ THE WAR
- ☐ KICKED IN THE HEAD BY A HORSE
- ☐ FIGHTING FIRE
- ☐ ILL TREATMENT BY HUSBAND
- ☐ IMAGINARY FEMALE TROUBLE
- ☐ HYSTERIA
- ☐ IMMORAL LIFE
- ☐ JEALOUSY AND RELIGION
- ☐ LAZINESS
- ☐ MENSTRUAL DERANGED
- ☐ NOVEL READING
- ☐ NYMPHOMANIA
- ☐ OPIUM HABIT
- ☐ EGOTISM
- ☐ HEREDITARY PREDISPOSITION

ATTACH PHOTO HERE

BEHAVIORAL STATUS

- ☐ COMPLAISANT
- ☐ AGGRAVATED
- ☐ DANGEROUS

MEDICATE IMMEDIATE-LY

ADMITTING DOCTOR